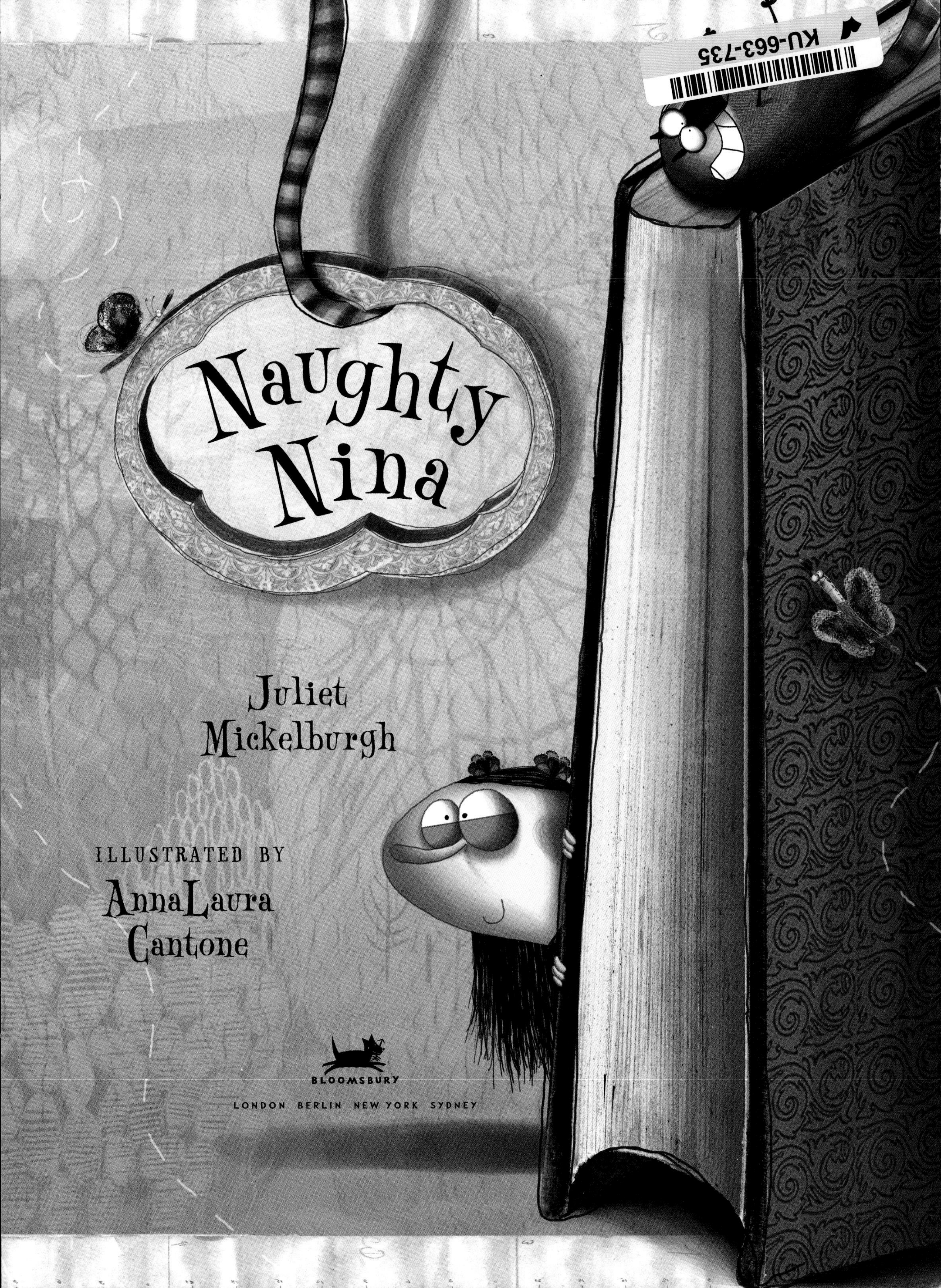

Naughty Nina

Juliet Mickelburgh

ILLUSTRATED BY
AnnaLaura Cantone

BLOOMSBURY
LONDON BERLIN NEW YORK SYDNEY

Nina was
nice.

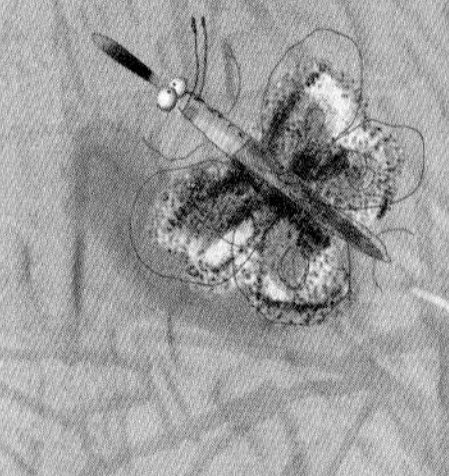

For Samo, Barty and Clemmie,
who are ever so nice and just a
little bit naughty, and for Moses,
who would have been if he could
– J.M.

For GretaOlivia, my perfect
little princess, just like Nina!
– A.C.

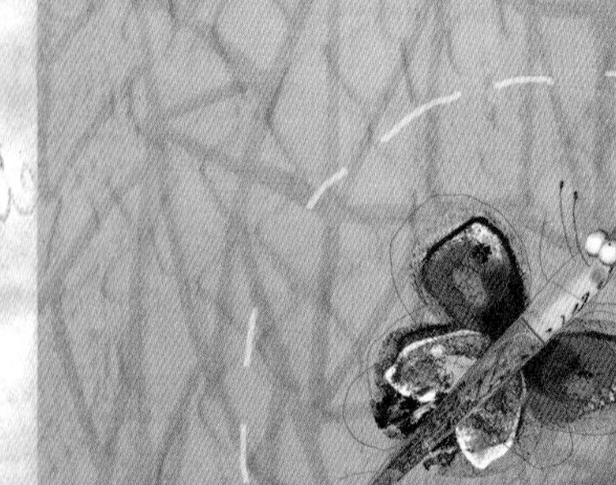

Bloomsbury Publishing, London, Berlin, New York and Sydney

First published in Great Britain in March 2011 by Bloomsbury Publishing Plc
36 Soho Square, London, W1D 3QY

A CIP catalogue record of this book is available from the British Library

ISBN 978 1 4088 0039 3

Printed in China

1 3 5 7 9 10 8 6 4 2

www.bloomsbury.com

Everybody said so.
'You're
SO NICE,
Nina,'
they said.

Nina did everything **nicely**.

Her paintings were **nice**.

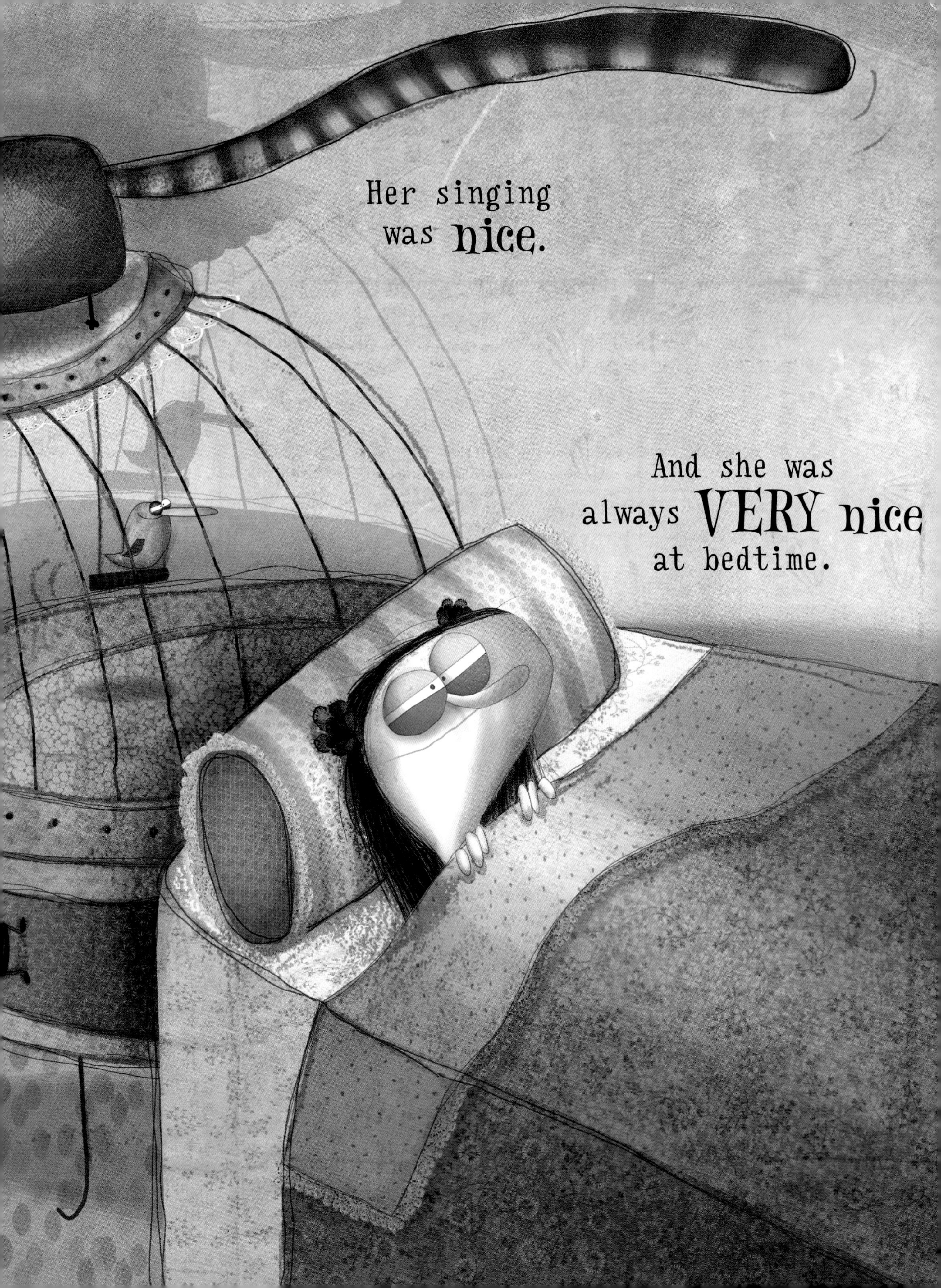

Her singing
was **nice**.

And she was
always **VERY nice**
at bedtime.

But Nina was bored
with being **nice**
all the time.

She wanted to be
a rascal and a
cheeky monkey and
get up to mischief.
She wanted
to be
NAUGHTY.

The more everybody said she was **nice**,
the less **nice** she felt.

Until one day she stopped
being **nice** altogether.

'I'm NOT NICE,
I'm NAUGHTY!'
she said.

She painted
all over
the walls.

She sang
all the
wrong notes.

And she was

VERY NAUGHTY

at bedtime.

Nina was
having fun.

Her parents
were not.
'Whatever has happened
to our **nice** Nina?'
they wailed.

Nina stuck
her tongue out.

Nina was
NAUGHTY
at school too.

She danced on
her desk.

She scribbled
in her books.

And she was
double trouble
in the
playground...

71

Nina was **really** having fun now.

Her teacher was not. 'Only **nice** girls get stickers,' said her teacher.

Nina didn't care.

Nina was
NAUGHTY
at tea with
Aunt Emily.

She blew bubbles
in her milkshake.

She talked
with her
mouth full.

And she didn't say
'please'
or
'thank you'.

Nina was having
the best fun
she'd ever had.

Aunt Emily was not.
'Where are your
nice
table manners,
young lady?'
she scolded.

Nina flicked
some jelly
with her spoon.

'I'm NOT NICE,
I'm NAUGHTY!'
she said.

Nina had been
NAUGHTY
once too often.

Now everybody said she was a
NAUGHTY little girl.
'You're SO NAUGHTY, Nina,'
they said.
And she was
sent to
her room.

Nina was
fed up.

She was bored
with being NAUGHTY
all the time.

She was bored
with being one thing...
...or the other.

'I just want
to be Nina,'
she said.

And so . . .
On most days
she helps around
the house.
She is usually
good as gold
at school.

She almost always
remembers her manners
at Aunt Emily's.

And she never
tries too hard
to be nice
or NAUGHTY
any more . . .

just to be Nina.

Three Little Ghosties
Pippa Goodhart
AnnaLaura Cantone
BLOOMSBURY PAPERBACKS
GLOW-IN-THE-DARK MOBILE INSIDE

By the same illustrator